INTRODUCTION
TO
FREEMASONRY

II Fellowcraft

Introduction to Freemasonry: II Fellowcraft
by Carl H. Claudy

ISBN: 1-59232-691-9

Printed in the United States of America

CARL. H. CLAUDY

INTRODUCTION
TO
FREEMASONRY

II Fellowcraft

CARL. H. CLAUDY

MUSIC

As battle-weary men long for the sea
  Like tired children, seeking Mother's breast,
  And in its restless endlessness find rest,
Its crashing surf a soothing systole;
As seeks the storm-tossed ship the harbor's lee,
  So mariners upon life's deep, hard-pressed
  To weather boiling trough and mounting crest,
Steer for the shelter of Freemasonry.
  Her ancient waves of sound lap on the strand,
    A melody more God's than man's. We hear,
      Like gentle murmurs in a curved sea shell
  Which whispers of some far off wonderland
    Where lightning flashes from blue skies and clear,
      The rolling thunder of the ritual.

INTRODUCTION TO FREEMASONRY

FELLOWCRAFT

As the Entered Apprentice Degree as a whole is symbolic of infancy and youth, a period of learning fundamentals, a beginning, so the Fellowcraft Degree is emblematic of manhood.

But it is a manhood of continued schooling; of renewed research; of further instruction. The Fellowcraft has passed his early Masonic youth, but he lacks the wisdom of age which he can attain only by use of the teachings of his first degree, broadened, strengthened, added to, by those experiences which come to men as distinguished from children.

Of the many symbols of this degree three stand out beyond all others as most beautiful and most important. They are the brazen Pillars; the Flight of Winding Stairs as a means of reaching the Middle Chamber by the teachings of the three, the five, and the seven steps; and the Letter "G" and all that it means to the Freemason.

Very obviously the Fellowcraft Degree is a call to learning, an urge to study, a glorification of education. Preston,[1] to whom we are indebted for much of the present form of this degree, evidently intended it as a foundation for that liberal education which in its classic form was so esteemed by the educated of Seventeenth and Eighteenth Century England. The explanations of the Five Orders of Architecture, the Five Senses and the Seven Liberal Arts and Sciences no longer embrace the essentials of a first-class education, but think not less of the degree on that account, since it is to be understood symbolically, not literally, as the great Masonic scholar may have intended.

While the degree contains moral teaching and a spiritual content only surpassed by that of the Sublime Degree, as a whole it is a call to books and study. If the Fellowcraft takes that to mean *Masonic* books and *Masonic* study he will find in this degree the touchstone which will make all three degrees a never-ending happiness for their fortunate possessor.

[1] William Preston, born 1742, died 1818. A most eminent Freemason of England who lived and labored during the formative Grand Lodge period. He was initiated in 1762. Later he became the Master of several lodges and was so interested in Freemasonry that he studied it deeply and wrote *Illustrations of Masonry*, a book to which historians and Masonic antiquarians are deeply indebted. After careful investigation he wrote the lectures of the several degrees, encouraged by the Grand Lodge, and later became its Deputy Grand Secretary. The Prestonian work used in the United States was modified and changed by Thomas Smith Webb, born 1771, died 1819. He was elected Grand Master in Rhode Island in 1813, but is best known for his *Freemasons Monitor*, or *Illustrations of Masonry*. Much of the printed ritual in United States jurisdictions is the same, or but little changed, from that first printed by Webb in 1797.

FELLOWCRAFT

Certain differences between this and the preceding degree are at once apparent. The Entered Apprentice about to be passed is no longer a candidate—he is a brother. In the first degree the candidate is received with a warning; in the second, the brother to be passed is received with an instruction. In the first degree the cable tow was for a physical purpose; here it is an aid, an urge to action, a girding up, a strengthening for the Masonic life to come. The circumambulation of the Fellowcraft is longer than that of the Apprentice: journey through manhood is longer than through youth. The obligation in the Entered Apprentice Degree stresses almost entirely the necessity for secrecy; in the Fellowcraft Degree secrecy is indeed enjoined upon the brother who kneels at the altar, but he also assumes duties toward his fellows and takes upon himself sacred obligations not intrusted to an Entered Apprentice. He learns of the pass, and he is poor in spirit indeed who is not thrilled to observe the slowly opening door which eventually will let in the whole effulgent Light of the East, typified by the position of the Square and Compasses upon the Volume of the Sacred Law.

A degree to muse upon and to study; one to see many, many times and still not come to the end of the great teachings here exemplified. Alas, too many brethren regard it as but a necessary stepping-stone between the solemnities of the Entered Apprentice's Degree and the glories of the Sublime Degree of Master Mason. Stepping-stone it is, indeed, but he uses it with difficulty and is assisted by it but little who cannot see behind its Pillars a rule of conduct for life; who cannot visualize climbing the Winding

Stairs as the pilgrimage we all must make; to whom the Middle Chamber is only a chamber in the middle and for whom the Letter "G" is but a letter.

CABLE TOW

The Fellowcraft wears it so that it may be an aid to his journey; by it a brother may assist him on his way. He also learns in this degree that a cable tow is more than a rope; it is at once a tie and a measurement.

How long is a cable tow? Thousands have asked and but a few have attempted to reply. In much older days it was generally considered to be three miles; that was when a brother was expected to attend lodge whether he wanted to or not if within the length of his cable tow.

Now we have learned that there is no merit in attendance which comes from fear of fines or other compulsion. The very rare but occasionally necessary summons may come to any Fellowcraft. When it comes, he must attend. But Freemasonry is not unreasonable. She does not demand the impossible, and she knows that what is easy for one is hard for another. To one brother ten miles away a summons may mean a call which he can answer only with great difficulty. To another several hundred miles away who has an airplane at his command it may mean no inconvenience.

Long before airplanes were thought of or railroad trains were anything but curiosities, it was determined (Baltimore Masonic Convention, 1843) that the length of a cable tow is "the scope of a brother's reasonable ability."

FELLOWCRAFT

Such a length the Fellowcraft may take to heart. Our gentle Fraternity compels no man against his will, leaving to each to determine for himself what is just and right and reasonable—and brotherly!

SPURIOUS

The use of two words in the Fellowcraft's Degree is a relic of antiquity and not a modern test to determine whether or not a Mason heles[1] the true word of a Fellowcraft. We have more accurate ways of knowing whether or not a would-be visitor comes from a legitimate or clandestine lodge[2] than his knowledge of ritual.

There are clandestine or spurious Masons, but they are not difficult to guard against. What all Fellowcrafts must be on watch to detect is any quality of spuriousness in their own Freemasonry. For there is no real Freemasonry of the lips only. A man may have a pocket full of dues cards showing that he is in good standing in a dozen different Masonic organizations; may be (although this is rare) a Past Master, and still, if he has not Freemasonry in his heart, be actually a spurious Mason.

[1] Hele: Masonically, rhymes with "fail." Often confused with "hail," a greeting or recognition. Hele (pronounced "hail") is to cover, to conceal. Is cognate with "cell," "hull," "hollow," "hell" (the covered place). In old provincial English, a "heler" was one who covered roofs with tiles or slates. Compare "tiler."

[2] Clandestine: other than recognized, not legitimate. A few clandestine Grand Lodges and subordinate bodies still exist in this country, organizations calling themselves Masonic but without descent from regular lodges or Grand Lodges, and without recognition by the Masonic world.

INTRODUCTION TO FREEMASONRY

Freemasonry is neither a thing nor a ritual. It is not a lodge nor an organization. Rather is it a manner of thought, a way of living, a guide to the City on a Hill. To make any less of it is to act as a spurious Mason. If the lesson of the pass as communicated in the degree means *this* to the Fellowcraft, then indeed has he the lesson of this part of the ceremony by heart.

GRAND LODGE

Every initiate should know something of the Grand Lodge, that august body which controls the Craft.

Before a Craft lodge can come into existence now there must be a Grand Lodge, the governing body of all the particular lodges, to give a warrant of constitution to at least seven brethren, empowering them to work and to be a Masonic lodge.

The age-old question which has plagued philosophers: did the first hen lay the first egg, or did the first egg hatch into the first hen, may seem to apply here, since before there can be a Grand Lodge there must be three or more private lodges to form it! But this is written of conditions in the United States to-day, not of those which obtained in 1717, when four individual lodges in London formed the first Grand Lodge.

To-day no regularly constituted lodge can come into being without the consent of an existing Grand Lodge. Most civilized countries now have Grand Lodges; the great formative period of Grand Lodges —the Eighteenth and Nineteenth centuries—is practically over. The vast majority of new lodges which will grow up as children of the mother will not form other Grand Lodges for themselves. It is not contended that no new Grand Lodges will ever be formed but only that less will come into being in the future than have in the past.[1]

The Grand Lodge, consisting of the particular lodges represented by their Masters, Senior, and Junior Wardens, and sometimes Past Masters, as well as the officers, Past Grand Masters and Past Grand Officers of the Grand Lodge, is the governing body in its jurisdiction. In the United States jurisdictional lines are coincident with state lines. Each Grand Jurisdiction is supreme unto itself; its word on any Masonic subject is Masonic law within its own borders.

A Grand Lodge adopts a constitution and by-laws for its government which is the body of the law of the Grand Judisdiction, which, however, rests upon the Old Charges and the Constitutions which have descended to us from the Mother Grand Lodge. The legal body is supplemented by the decisions made by Grand Masters, or the Grand Lodge, or both, general regulations, laws, resolutions and edicts of the Grand Lodge, all in accord with the "ancient usages and customs of the Fraternity."

In the interim between meetings of a Grand Lodge the Grand Master is the Grand Lodge. His powers are arbitrary and great but not unlimited. Most Grand Lodges provide that certain acts of the Grand Master may be revised, confirmed or rejected by the Grand Lodge as a check upon any too radical

[1] When and if a forty-ninth State is admitted to the Union, doubtless it will have its own Grand Lodge.

moves. But a brother rarely becomes a Grand Master without serving a long and arduous apprenticeship. Almost invariably he has been Master of his own lodge and by years of service and interest demonstrated his ability and his fitness to preside over the Grand Lodge. The real check against arbitrary actions of a Grand Master is more in his Masonry than the law, more in his desire to do right than in the legal power compelling him to do so.

Most Grand Lodges meet once a year for business, election, and installation of officers. Some Grand Lodges (Massachusetts and Pennsylvania, for instance) meet in quarterly communications. All Grand Lodges meet in special communications at the call of the Grand Master.

The Grand Lodge receives and disburses certain funds; these come as dues from the constituent lodges, from gifts and bequests, from special assessments, etc. The funds are spent as the Grand Lodge orders; upon charity, the maintenance of the Home, the expenses of the Grand Lodge, maintaining a Grand Secretary and his office and staff, publication of Proceedings, educational work, etc.

Most Grand Lodges also publish a manual or monitor of the non-secret work of the degrees which may or may not also contain the forms for various Masonic ceremonies such as dedication of lodge halls, cornerstone laying, funeral service, etc. Most Grand Lodges also publish a Digest or Code, which contains the constitution, by-laws, and regulations of the Grand Lodge, and the resolutions, edicts, and decisions under which the Craft works. The interested Mason will procure these at his earliest convenience that he may be well informed regarding the laws and customs of his own jurisdiction.

WORKING TOOLS

The working tools of a Fellowcraft are the Plumb, the Square, and the Level. The Entered Apprentice has learned of them as the Immovable Jewels, but in the Fellowcraft's Degree they have a double significance. They are still the Jewels of the three principal officers, still immovably fixed in the East, the West, and the South, but they are also given into the hands of the Fellowcraft with instructions the more impressive for their brevity.

The tools represent an advance in knowledge. The Entered Apprentice received a Twenty-four Inch Gauge and a Common Gavel with which to measure and lay out a rough ashlar and chip off its edges to fit a stone ready for the builders' use. But that is all he may do. Not with gauge or gavel may be build; only prepare material for another. He is still but a beginner, a student; to his hands are intrusted only such tasks as if ill done will not materially affect the whole.

The Fellowcraft uses the Plumb, the Square, and the Level. With the Square he tests the work of the Apprentice; with the Level he lays the courses of the wall he builds; with the Plumb he raises perpendicular columns. If he use his tools aright he demonstrates that he is worthy to be a Fellow of the Craft and no Apprentice; that he can lay a wall and build a tower which will stand.

Hence the symbolism of the three tools as taught

in the monitorial work. The Plumb admonishes us to walk uprightly; that is, not leaning over, not awry with the world or ourselves, but straight and square with the base of life on which we tread. We are to square our actions by the Square of Virtue. Every man has a conscience, be it ever so dead; every Freemason is expected to carry the conscience of a Fellowcraft's Square of Virtue in his breast and build no act, no matter how small, which does not fit within its right angle.

The operative Fellow of the Craft builds his wall course by course, each level and straight. We build upon the level of time, a fearsome level indeed. The Fellow of the Craft whose wall stands not true on a physical level may take down his stones, retemper his mortar and try again. But the Freemason can never unbuild that which is erected on the level of time; once gone, the opportunity is gone forever. Omar said, "The moving finger writes, and having writ, *moves on.*" The poet Oxenham phrased it . . . "No man travels *twice* the great highway which winds through darkness up to light, through night, to day."

Therefore does it behoove the Fellowcraft to build on his level of time with a true Plumb and a right Square.

In its interweaving of emblem with emblem, teaching with teaching, symbol with symbol, Freemasonry is like the latticework atop the Pillars in the Porch of King Solomon's Temple, the several parts of which are so intimately connected as to denote unity. Here the Plumb as a Jewel, the Plumb as a working tool of the Fellowcraft, and the Heavenly Plumb in the hand of Jehovah, as told in Amos vii, are so inextricably mingled that while references to them occur in different parts of the degree, symbolically they must be considered together.

"AMOS, WHAT SEEST THOU?"

Thus he shewed me; and behold the Lord stood upon a wall made by a plumb line, with a plumb line in his hand. And the Lord said unto me, Amos, what seest thou? And I said, a plumb line. Then said the Lord, Behold, I will set a plumb line in the midst of my people Israel; I will not again pass by them any more.

This passage from the Great Light is as much a part of the ritual of the Fellowcraft's Degree as the 133rd Psalm is of the Entered Apprentice's Degree, and has the same intimate connection with the teachings of this ceremony.

The vital and important part is this: the Lord set a plumb line *in the midst of his people Israel.* He did not propose to judge them by a plumb line afar off in another land, in high heaven, but here—here in the midst of them.

This is of intense interest to the Fellowcraft Mason, since it teaches him how he should judge his own work—and, more important, how he should judge the work of others.

Presumably plumb lines hang alike. Presumably all plumbs, like all squares and all levels, are equally accurate. Yet a man may use a tool thinking it accurate which to another is not true. If the tool of building and the tool of judging be not alike either the judgment must be inaccurate or the judge must take into consideration the tool by which the work was done.

By the touch system, a blind man may learn to write upon a typewriter. If a loosened type drops from the type bar when the blind man strikes the letter "e" he will make but a little black smudge upon the paper. It is perfectly legible; in this sentence every "e" but one has been smudged. Would you criticize the blind man for imperfect work? He has no means of knowing that his tool is faulty. If you found the smudges which stand for the letter "e" in the right places, showing that he had used his imperfect machine perfectly, would you not consider that he had done perfect work? Aye, because you would judge by a plumb line "in the midst" of the man and his work. If, however, the paper with the smudged letters "e" were judged by one who knew nothing of the workman's blindness, nothing of his typewriter, one who saw only a poor piece of typing, doubtless he would judge it as imperfect.

The builders of the Washington monument and the Eiffel Tower in Paris both used plumb lines accurate to the level of the latitude and longitude of these structures. Both are at right angles with sea level. Yet to some observer on the moon equipped with a strong telescope these towers would not appear parallel. As they are in different latitudes they rise from the surface of the earth at an angle to each other.

Doubtless he who engineered the monument would protest that the monument to Washington was right and the French engineer's tower wrong. The Frenchman, knowing his plumb was accurate, would believe the monument crooked. But the Great Architect, we may hope, would think *both* right knowing each was perfect by the plumb by which it was erected.

The Fellowcraft learns to judge his work by his own plumb line, not by another's; if he erects that which is good work, true work, square work by his own working tools—in other words, by his own standards—he does well. Only when a Fellowcraft is false to his own conscience is he building other than fair and straight.

CORN, WINE, AND OIL

The wages which our ancient brethren received for their labors in the building of King Solomon's Temple are paid no more. We use them only as symbols, save in the dedication, constitution, and consecration of a new lodge and in the laying of cornerstones, when once again the fruit of the land, the brew of the grape and the essence of the olive are poured to launch a new unit of brotherhood into the fellowship of lodges; to begin a new structure dedicated to public or Masonic use.

In the Great Light are many references to these particular forms of wealth. In ancient days the grapes in the vineyard, the olives in the grove and the grain of the field were not only wealth but the measure of trade; so many skins of wine, so many cruses of oil, so many bushels of corn were then as are dollars and cents to-day. Thus when our ancient brethren received wages in corn, wine, and oil they were paid for their labors in coin of the realm.

The oil pressed from the olive was as important to the Jews in Palestine as butter and other fats are among Occidentals. Because it was so necessary and hence so valuable it became an important part of sacrificial rites.

Oil was also used not only as a food but for lighting purposes within the house, not in the open air where the torch was more effective. Oil was also an article of the toilet; mixed with perfume it was used in the ceremonies of anointment and in preparation for ceremonial appearances. The "precious ointment which ran down upon the beard, even Aaron's beard" was doubtless made of olive oil suitably mixed with such perfumes and spices as myrrh, cinnamon, galbanum and frankincense. Probably oil was also used as a surgical dressing; nomadic peoples, subject to injuries, could hardly avoid knowledge of the value of soothing oil.

The corn of the Old Testament is not the corn we know. In the majority of the uses of the word a more understandable translation would be "grain." The principal grains of the Old Testament days were barley and wheat and "corn" represents not only both of these but all the grains which the Jews cultivated.

An ear of grain has been an emblem of plenty since the mists of antiquity shrouded the beginnings of mythology. Ceres, goddess of abundance, survives to-day in our cereals. The Greeks called her Demeter, a corruption of Gemeter, our mother earth. She wore a garland of grain and carried ears of grain in her hand.

The Hebrew *Shibboleth* means both an ear of corn

and a flood of water. Both are symbols of abundance, plenty, wealth.

Scarcely less important to our ancient brethren than their corn and oil was wine. Vineyards were highly esteemed both as wealth and as comfort—the pleasant shade of the vine and fig tree was a part of ancient hospitality. Vineyards on mountain sides or hills were most carefully tended and protected against washing by terraces and walls, as even to-day one may see on the hillsides of the Rhine. Thorn hedges kept cattle from the grapes. The vineyardist frequently lived in a watchtower or hut on an elevation to keep sharp look out that neither predatory man nor beast took his ripening wealth.

Thus corn, wine, and oil were the wages of a Fellowcraft in the days of King Solomon. Freemasons receive no material wages for their labors, but if the work done in a lodge is paid for only in coin of the heart such wages are no less real. They may sustain as does the grain, refresh as does the wine, give joy and gladness as does the oil. How much we receive, what we do with our wages, depends entirely on our Masonic work. Our ancient brethren were paid for their physical labors. Whether their wages were paid for work performed upon the mountains and in the quarries, or whether they received corn, wine, and oil because they labored in the fields and vineyards, it was true then and it is true now that only "in the sweat of thy face shalt thou eat bread." To receive the Masonic equivalent of the ancient corn, wine, and oil, a brother must labor. He must till the fields of his own heart or build the temple of his own house not made with hands. He must give labor to his neighbor or carry stones for his brother's temple.

If he stand and wait and watch and wonder, he will not be able to ascend into the Middle Chamber where our ancient brethren received their wages. If he works for the joy of working, does his part in his lodge work, takes his place among the laborers of Freemasonry, he will receive corn, wine, and oil in measures pressed down and running over and know a fraternal joy as substantial in fact as it is ethereal in quality; as real in his heart as it is intangible to the profane world.

For all Fellowcrafts—aye, for all Freemasons—corn, wine, and oil are symbols of sacrifice, of the fruits of labor, of wages earned.

THE TWO PILLARS

And King Solomon sent and fetched Hiram out of Tyre. He was a widow's son of the tribe of Naphtali,[1] *and his father was a man of Tyre, a worker in brass; and he was filled with wisdom, and understanding, and cunning to work all works in brass. And he came to King Solomon, and wrought all his work. For he cast two pillars of brass, of eighteen cubits*[2] *high apiece; and a line of twelve cubits did compass either of them about. . . .*

And he set up the pillars in the porch of the temple; and he set up the right pillar, and called the name thereof Jachin; and he set up the left pillar, and called the name thereof Boaz. And upon the top

[1] Pronounced Naf'tal-i.
[2] A cubit is approximately 18 inches.

of the pillars was lily work; so was the work of the pillars finished. (I Kings vii, 13–22.)

Also he made before the house two pillars of thirty and five cubits high, and the chapiter that was on the top of each of them was five cubits. And he made chains, as in the oracle, and put them on the heads of the pillars and made an hundred pomegranates and put them on the chains. (II Chronicles iii, 15–16.)

From the dawn of religion the pillar, monolith or built-up, has played an important part in the worship of the Unseen. From the huge boulders of Stonehenge, among which the Druids are supposed to have performed their rites, through East Indian temples to the religion of ancient Egypt, scholars trace the use of pillars as an essential part of religious worship; indeed, in Egypt the obelisk stood for the very presence of the Sun God himself.

It is not strange, then, that Hiram of Tyre should erect pillars for Solomon's Temple. What has seemed strange is the variation in the dimensions given in Kings and Chronicles; a discrepancy which is explained by the theory that Kings gives the height of one and Chronicles of both pillars together.

Of the ritualistic explanation of the two brazen pillars it is not necessary to speak at length, since the Middle Chamber lecture is quite satisfyingly explicit regarding their ancient use and purpose. But their inner symbolic significance is not touched upon in the ritual; it is one of the hidden beauties of Freemasonry left for each brother to hunt down for himself.

It is a poor symbol that has but one meaning. Of

the many interpretations of the Brazen Pillars, two are here selected as vivid and important.

The ancients believed the earth to be flat and that it was supported by two Pillars of God, placed at the western entrance of the world as then known. These are now called Gibraltar, on one side of the Strait, and Ceuta on the other. This may account for the origin of the twin pillars. However this may be, the practice of erecting columns at the entrance of an edifice dedicated to worship prevailed in Egypt and Phœnicia, and at the erection of King Solomon's Temple the Brazen Pillars were placed in the porch thereof.

Some writers have suggested that they represent the masculine and feminine elements in nature; others, that they stand for the authority of Church and State, because on stated occasions the high priest stood before one pillar and the king before the other. Some students think that they allude to the two legendary pillars of Enoch, upon which, tradition informs us, all the wisdom of the ancient world was inscribed in order to preserve it from inundations and conflagrations. William Preston supposed that, by them, Solomon had reference to the pillars of cloud and fire which guided the Children of Israel out of bondage and up to the Promised Land. One authority says a literal translation of their names is: "In Thee is strength," and, "It shall be established," and by a natural transposition may be thus expressed: "Oh, Lord, Thou art almighty and Thy power is established from everlasting to everlasting."

It is impossible to escape the conviction that in meaning they are related to religion, and represent the strength and stability, the perpetuity and providence of God, and in Freemasonry are symbols of a living faith.

Faith cannot be defined. The factors of mightiest import cannot be caught up in speech. Life is the primary fact of which we are conscious, and yet there is no language by which it can be fenced in. No chart can be made of a mother's love; it is deeper than words and reads in little, common things a wealth that is more than golden.

While we cannot define, we can recognize the power of faith. It generates energy. It is the dynamics of elevated characters and noble spirits, the source of all that bears the impress of greatness.

And we can realize its necessity. Without faith it would be impossible to transact business. "It spans the earth with railroads, and cleaves the sea with ships. It gives man wings to fly the air, and fins to swim the deep. It creates the harmony of music and the whir of factory wheels. It draws man up toward the angels and brings heaven down to earth." By it all human relationship is conditioned. We must have faith in institutions and ideals, faith in friendship, family and fireside, faith in self, faith in man, and faith in God.

Freemasonry is the oldest, the largest, and the most widely distributed fraternal Order on the face of the earth to-day by reason of its faith in God. At one end of the Second Section of the Fellowcraft Degree are the Two Brazen Pillars—a symbol of that faith; at its other end is the Letter "G," a living sign of the same belief.

But there is another interpretation of the symbolism.

The Entered Apprentice in process of being passed to the degree of Fellowcraft *passes between the pillars.* No hint is given that he should pass nearer to one than to the other; no suggestion is made that either may work a greater influence than the other. He merely passes between.

A deep significance is in this very omission. Masons refer to the promise of God unto David; the interested may read Chapter vii of II Samuel for themselves, and gather that the establishment promised by the Lord was that of a house, a family, a descent of blood from David unto his children and his children's children.

The pillars were named by Hiram Abif; those names have many translations. Strength and establishment are but two; power, and wisdom or control, fit the meaning of the words as well.

Used to blast stumps from fields dynamite is an aid to the farmer. Used in war it kills and maims. Fire cooks our food and makes steam for our engines; fire also burns up our houses and destroys our forests. But it is not the power but the use of power which is good or bad. The truth applies to any power; spiritual, legal, monarchial, political, personal. Power is without either virtue or vice; the user may use it well or ill, as he pleases.

Freemasonry passes the brother in process of becoming a Fellowcraft between the pillar of strength—power; and the pillar of establishment—choice or control. He is a man now and no minor or infant. He has grown up Masonically. Before him are spread the two great essentials to all success, all greatness, all happiness.

FELLOWCRAFT

Like any other power—temporal or physical, religious or spiritual—Freemasonry can be used well or ill. Here is the lesson set before the Fellowcraft; if he like David would have his kingdom of Masonic manhood established in strength he must pass between the pillars with understanding that power without control is useless, and control without power, futile. Each is a complement of the other; in the passage between the pillars the Fellowcraft not only has his feet set upon the Winding Stairs but is given—so he has eyes to see and ears to hear—secret instructions as to how he shall climb those stairs that he may, indeed, reach the Middle Chamber. He shall climb by strength, but directed by wisdom; he shall progress by power, but guided by control; he shall rise by the might that is in him, but arrive by the wisdom of his heart.

So seen the pillars become symbols of high value; the initiate of old saw in the obelisk the very spirit of the God he worshiped. The modern Masonic initiate may see in them both the faith and the means by which he may travel a little further, a little higher toward the secret Middle Chamber of life in which dwells the Unseen Presence.

THE GLOBES

The "world celestial and the world terrestrial" on the brazen pillars were added by comparatively modern ritual makers. Solomon knew them not, although contemporaries of Solomon believed the earth stood still while a hollow sphere with its inner surface dotted with stars revolved about the earth. The slowly turning celestial sphere is as old as mankind's observations of the starry decked heavens.

It is to be noted that both terrestrial and celestial spheres are used as emblems of universality. This is not mere duplication for emphasis; each teaches an individual part of universality. What is called universal on the earth—as for instance the necessity of mankind to breathe, drink water and eat in order to live—is not necessarily universal in all the universe. We have no knowledge that any other planet in our solar system is inhabited—what evidence there is is rather to the contrary. We are ignorant of any other sun which has any inhabited planets in its system. If life does exist in some world to us unknown, it may be entirely different from life on this planet. A symbol of universality which applied only to the earth would be a self-contradiction.

Real universality means what it says. It appertains to the whole universe. A Mason's charity of relief to the poor and distressed must obviously be confined to this particular planet, but his charity of thought may, so we are taught, extend "through the boundless realms of eternity."

The world terrestrial and the world celestial on our representations of the pillars, in denoting universality, mean that the principles of our Order are not founded upon mere earthly conditions and transient truths, but rest upon divine and limitless foundations, coexistent with the cosmos and its Creator.

THE WINDING STAIRS

Like so much else in Freemasonry the Middle Chamber is wholly symbolic. It seems obvious that

Solomon the Wise would not have permitted any practice so time wasting and uneconomic as sending many thousand workmen up a flight of stairs to a small Middle Chamber to receive corn, wine, and oil which had to be brought up in advance, only to be carried down in small lots by each workman as he received his wages.

If we are to accept the Scriptural account of the Temple as accurate, there actually were winding stairs. "And they went up with winding stairs into the middle chamber" is stated in I Kings. That the stairs had the three, five, and seven steps by which we rise is not stated in the Scriptures. Only in this country have the Winding Stairs fifteen steps. In older days the stairs had but five, sometimes seven steps. Preston had thirty-six steps in his Winding Stairs in a series of one, three, five, seven, nine, and eleven. But this violated a Pythagorean principle—and Freemasonry has adopted much in its system from the science of numbers as exemplified by Pythagoras as the Fellowcraft will discover when—if—he receives the Sublime Degree.

The great philosopher Pythagoras taught that odd numbers were more perfect than even; indeed, the temple builders who wrought long before Pythagoras always built their stairs with an odd number of steps, so that, starting with the right foot at the bottom the climber might enter the sacred place at the top with the same foot in advance. Freemasonry uses only odd numbers, with particular reliance on three: three degrees, three principal officers, three steps, three Lesser Lights, and so on.

Hence the English system later eliminated the

number eleven from Preston's thirty-six, making twenty-five steps in all.

The stairs as a whole are a representation of life; not the physical life of eating, drinking, sleeping and working, but the mental and spiritual life, of both the lodge and the world without; of learning, studying, enlarging mental horizons, increasing the spiritual outlook. Freemasons divide the fifteen steps into three, referring to the officers of a lodge; five, concerned with the orders of architecture and the human senses; and seven, the Liberal Arts and Sciences.

THE NUMBER THREE

The first three steps represent the three principal officers of a lodge, and—though not stated in the ritual—must always refer to Deity, of which *three*, the triangle, is the most ancient symbol.

Their principal implication here is to assure the Fellowcraft just starting his ascent that he does not climb alone. The Worshipful Master, Senior, and Junior Wardens are themselves symbolic of the lodge as a whole, and thus (as a lodge is a symbol of the world) of the Masonic world—the Fraternity. The Fellowcraft is surrounded by the Craft. The brethern are present to help him climb. In his search for truth, in his quest of his wages in the Middle Chamber, the Fellowcraft is to receive the support and assistance of all in the Mystic Circle; surely an impressive symbol.

If we examine a little into the powers and duties of the Worshipful Master and his Wardens, we may see how they rule and govern the lodge and so by what means they may aid the Fellowcraft in his ascent.

WORSHIPFUL[1] MASTER

The incumbent of the Oriental Chair has powers peculiar to his station which are far greater than those of the president of a society or the chairman of a meeting of any kind. President and chairman are elected by the body over which they preside and may be removed by that body. A Master is elected by his lodge but can be removed only by the Grand Master (or his Deputy acting for him) or Grand Lodge. The presiding officer is bound by the rules of order adopted by the body and by its by-laws. A lodge cannot pass by-laws to alter, amend, or curtail the inherent powers of a Master.

Grand Lodges so differ in their interpretation of some of the "ancient usages and customs" of the Fraternity that what applies in one jurisdiction does not necessarily apply in another. But certain powers of a Master are so well recognized that they may be considered universal.

[1] Worshipful: greatly respected. The Wycliffe Bible (Matthew xix, 19) reads: "Worschip thi fadir and thi modir." The Authorized Version translates "worschip" to "honor"—"honor thy father and thy mother." In parts of England to-day one hears the Mayor spoken of as *Worshipful*, the word used in its ancient sense, meaning one worthy, honorable, to be respected. "Worshipful" as applied to the Master of a lodge does not mean that we should bow down to him in adoration as when used in its ecclesiastical sense. We "worship" God, but not men. Our Masters in being called "Worshipful" are but paid a tribute of respect in the language of two or more centuries ago.

The Master may congregate his lodge when he pleases and for what purpose he wishes, *provided* it does not interfere with the laws of the Grand Lodge. For instance, he may assemble his lodge at a special communication to confer degrees, at his pleasure; but he must not disobey that requirement of the Grand Lodge which calls for proper notice to the brethren, nor may a Master confer a degree in less than the statutory time following a preceding degree without a dispensation from the Grand Master.

The Master has the right of presiding over and governing his lodge, and only the Grand Master or his Deputy may suspend him. He may put any brother in the East to preside or to confer a degree; he may then resume the gavel at his pleasure—even in the middle of a sentence! But when he has delegated authority temporarily the Master is not relieved from responsibility for what occurs in his lodge.

It is the Master's right to control lodge business and work. It is in a very real sense *his* lodge. He decides all points of order and no appeal from his decision may be taken to the lodge. He can initiate and terminate debate at his pleasure and can propose or second any motion. He may open and close the lodge at his pleasure, except that he may not open a stated communication earlier than the hour stated in the by-laws. He is responsible only to the Grand Master and the Grand Lodge, the obligations he assumed when he was installed,[1] his conscience, and his God.

[1] Officers are seated in their chairs and assume the powers of their offices by a ceremony of installation, following election or appointment.

FELLOWCRAFT

The Master has the right to say who may enter and who may leave the lodge room. He may deny a visitor entrance; but he must have a good and sufficient reason, otherwise his Grand Lodge will unquestionably rule such a drastic step arbitrary and punish accordingly. *Per contra,* if he permits the entry of a visitor to whom some member has objected, he may also subject himself to Grand Lodge discipline. In other words his *power* to admit or exclude a visitor is absolute; his *right* to admit or exclude a visitor is hedged about by the pledges he takes at his installation and the rules of his Grand Lodge.

A very important power of a Master is that of appointing committees. No lodge may appoint a committee. The lodge may pass a resolution that a committee be appointed, but the selection of that committee is an inherent right of the Master. He is *ex officio* a member of all committees he appoints. The reason is obvious; he is responsible to the Grand Master and the Grand Lodge for the conduct of his lodge. If the lodge could appoint committees and act upon their recommendations, the Master would be in the anomalous position of having great responsibilities, but no power to carry out their performance.

Only the Master may order a committee to examine a visiting brother. It is his responsibility to see that no cowan or eavesdropper comes within the tiled door. Therefore it is for him to pick a committee in which he has confidence. So, also, with the committees which report upon petitioners. He is responsible for the accuracy, the fair-mindedness, the speed and the intelligence of such investigations. It is, therefore, for him to say to whom shall be delegated this necessary and important work.

It is generally, not exclusively, held that only a Master can issue a summons. In a few jurisdictions the lodge members present at a stated communication may summons the whole membership.

If he keeps within the laws, resolutions, and edicts of his Grand Lodge on the one hand, and the Landmarks, Old Charges, Constitutions and ancient usages and customs on the other, the power of the Worshipful Master is that of an absolute monarch. His responsibilities and his duties are those of an apostle of Light!

THE WARDENS

Wardens are found in all bodies of Masonry, in all rites, in all countries.

Its derivation gives the meaning of the word. It comes from the Saxon *weardian*, to guard, to watch. In France the second and third officers are *premier* and *second Surveillant;* in Germany *erste* and *zwite Aufseher;* in Spain *primer* and *segundo Vigilante;* in Italy *primo* and *secondo Sorvegliante*, all the words meaning one who overlooks, watches, keeps ward, observes.

Whether the title came from the provision of the old rituals that the Wardens sit beside the two pillars in the porch of the temple to oversee or watch, the Senior Warden the Fellowcrafts and the Junior Warden the Apprentices, or whether the old rituals were developed from the custom of the Middle Ages Guilds having Wardens (watchers) is a moot question.

FELLOWCRAFT

In the French Rite and the Scottish Rite both Wardens sit in the West near the columns. In the Blue Lodge the symbolism is somewhat impaired by the Junior Warden sitting in the South, but is strengthened by giving each Warden, as an emblem of authority, a replica of the column beneath the shade of which he once sat. The column of the Senior Warden is erect, that of the Junior Warden on its side, while the lodge is at labor. During refreshment the Senior Warden's column is laid prostrate while that of the Junior Warden is erected, so that by a glance at either South or West the Craft may know at all times whether the lodge is at labor or refreshment.

The government of the Craft by a Master *and two Wardens* cannot be too strongly emphasized. It is not only the right but the duty of the Senior Warden to assist the Worshipful Master in opening and governing his lodge. When he uses it to enforce orders, his setting maul or gavel is to be respected; he has a proper officer to carry his messages to the Junior Warden or elsewhere; under the Master he is responsible for the conduct of the lodge while at labor.

The Junior Warden's duties are less important; he observes the time and calls the lodge from labor to refreshment and refreshment to labor in due season at the orders of the Master. It is his duty to see that "none of the Craft convert the purposes of refreshment into intemperance and excess" which doubtless has a bibulous derivation, coming from days when refreshment meant wine. If we no longer drink wine at lodge, we still have reason for this charge upon the Junior Warden, since it is his unpleasant duty, when ordered by the Master or Grand Master, because he supervises the conduct of the Craft at refreshment, to prefer charges against those suspected of Masonic misconduct.

Only Wardens (or Past Masters) may be elected Master. This requirement (which has certain exceptions, as in the formation of a new lodge) is very old. The fourth of the Old Charges reads:

> No brother can be a Warden until he has passed the part of a Fellowcraft;[1] nor a Master, until he has acted as Warden; nor Grand Warden, until he has been Master of a Lodge; nor Grand Master, unless he has been a Fellowcraft before his election.

The Warden's is a high and exalted office; his duties are many, his responsibilities great; his powers only exceeded by those of the Master.

THE NUMBER FIVE

Five has always been a sacred and mystical number; Pythagoras made of it a symbol of life, since it rejected unity by the addition of the first even and the first odd number. It was therefore symbolic of happiness and misery, birth and death, order and disorder—in other words, life as it was lived. Egypt knew five minor planets, five elements, five elementary powers. The Greeks had four elements and added ether, the unknown, making a cosmos of five.

[1] At the time of the formation of the Mother Grand Lodge in London (1717) the Fellowcrafts formed the body of Masonry, as Master Masons do to-day.

FELLOWCRAFT

Five is peculiarly the number of the Fellowcraft's Degree; it represents the central group of the three which form the stairs; it refers to the five orders of architecture; five are required to hold a Fellowcraft's Lodge; there are five human senses; geometry is the fifth science, and so on.

In the Winding Stairs the number five represents first the five orders of architecture.

ARCHITECTURE

Here for the first time the initiate is introduced to the science of building as a whole. He has been presented with working tools; he has had explained the rough and perfect ashlars, he has heard of the house not made with hands; he knows something of the building of the Temple. Now he is taught of architecture as a science; its beginnings are laid before him; he is shown how the Greeks commenced and the Romans added to the kinds of architecture; he learns of the beautiful, perfect and complete whole which is a well-designed, well-constructed building.

Here is symbolism in quantity! And here indeed the Fellowcraft gets a glimpse of all that Freemasonry may mean to a man, for just as the Freemasons of old were the builders of the cathedrals and the temples for the worship of the Most High, so is the Speculative Freemason pledged to the building of his spiritual temple.

Temples are built stone by stone, a little at a time. Each stone must be hewn from the solid rock of the quarry. Then it must be laid out and chipped with the gavel until it is a perfect ashlar. Finally it must be set in place with the tempered mortar which will bind. But before any stone may be placed, a plan must come into existence; the architect must plan his part. As the Fellowcraft hears in the degree:

> A survey of nature, and the observation of her beautiful proportions, first induced man to imitate the divine plan, and to study symmetry and order. This gave rise to society, and birth to every useful art. The architect began to design, and the plans which he laid down, improved by time and experience, have led to the production of works which are the admiration of every age.

So must the Fellowcraft, studying the orders of architecture by which he will erect his spiritual temple, design the structure before he commences to build.

There are *five* orders of architecture, not one. There are many plans on which a man may build a life, not one only. Freemasonry does not attempt to distinguish as between the Doric, Ionic, and Corinthian as to beauty or desirability. She does suggest that the Tuscan, plainer than the Doric, and the Composite, more ornamental though not more beautiful than the Corinthian, are less reverenced than the ancient and original orders. Freemasonry makes no attempt to influence the Fellowcraft as to which order of life building he shall choose. He may elect the physical, the mental, the spiritual. Or he may choose the sacrificial—"plainer than the Doric"—or the ornamental, which is "not more beautiful than the Corinthian." Freemasonry is concerned less with what order of spiritual architecture a Fellowcraft chooses by which to build than that he does choose one; that he build not aimlessly. He is bidden to study symmetry and order.

Architecture is perhaps the most beautiful and expressive of all the arts. Painting and sculpture, noble though they are, lack the utility of architecture and strive to interpret nature rather than to originate. Architecture is not hampered by the necessity of reproducing something already in existence. It may raise its spires untrammeled by any nature model; it may fling its arches gloriously across a nave and transept with no similitude in nature to hamper by suggestion. If his genius be great enough, the architect may tell in his structure truths which may not be put in words, inspire by glories not sung in the divinest harmonies.

So may the builder of his own house not made with hands, if he choose aright his plan of life and hew to the line of his plan. So, indeed, have done all those great men who have led the world; the prophets of old, Pythagoras, Confucius, Buddha, Shakespeare, Milton, Goethe, Washington, Lincoln . . .

THE FIVE SENSES

If the Fellowcraft, climbing his three, five, and seven steps to a Middle Chamber of unknown proportions, containing an unknown wage, is overweighted with the emphasis put upon the spiritual side of life, he may here be comforted.

Freemasonry is not an ascetic organization. It recognizes that the physical is as much a part of normal life as the mental and spiritual upon which so much emphasis is put.

The Fellowcraft Degree is a glorification of education, the gaining of knowledge, the study of the Seven Liberal Arts and Sciences and all that they connote. Therefore it is wholly logical that the degree should make special reference to the five means by which man has acquired all his knowledge; aye, by which he will ever acquire any knowledge.

All learning is sense-bound. Inspiring examples have been given the world by unfortunates deprived of one or more senses. Blind men often make as great a success as those who see; deaf men often overcome the handicap until it appears nonexistent. Helen Keller is blind, deaf, and was dumb as well; all that she has accomplished—and it would be a great accomplishment with all five senses—has been done through feeling and tasting and smelling.

But take away *all* five senses and a man is no more a man; perhaps his mind is no more a mind. With no contact whatever with the material world he can learn nothing of it. As man reaches up through the material to the spiritual, he could learn nothing of ethics without contact with the physical.

If there are limits beyond which human investigations and explorations into the unknown may not go, it is because of the limitations of the five senses. Not even the extension of those senses by the marvelously sensitive instruments of science may overcome, in the last analysis, their limits.

Some objects are smaller than any rays we know except X-rays. If it were possible to construct a microscope powerful enough to see an atom, the only light by which it could be seen would be X-rays. But the very X-rays which would be necessary to see it would destroy the atom as soon as they struck it. In our present knowledge, then, to see the atom is beyond the power of human senses. If anything is beyond the power of eyes, even if aided by the greatest magnification, then there must be truths beyond the power of touch and taste and smell and hearing, regardless of the magnification science may provide.

Except for one factor! Brute beasts hear, see, feel, smell, and taste, as do we. But they garner no facts of science, win no truths, formulate no laws of nature through these senses. More than the five senses are necessary to perceive the relation between thing and thing, and life and life. That factor is the perception, the mind, the soul or spirit, if you will, which differentiates man from all other living beings.

If the Fellowcraft's five steps, then, seem to glorify the five senses of human nature, it is because Freemasonry is a well-rounded scheme of life and living which recognizes the physical as well as the mental life of men and knows that only through the physical do we perceive the spiritual. It is in this sense, not as a simple lesson in physiology, that we are to receive the teachings of the five steps by which we rise above the ground floor of the Temple to that last flight of seven steps which are typical of knowledge.

THE NUMBER SEVEN

Most potent of numbers in the ancient religions, the number seven has deep significance. The Pythagoreans called it the perfect number, as made up of three and four, the two perfect figures, triangle and square. It was the virgin number because it cannot be multiplied to produce any number within ten, as can two and two, two and three, and two and four, three and three. Nor can it be produced by the multiplication of any whole numbers.

Our ancient ancestors knew seven planets, seven Pleiades, seven Hyades, and seven lights burned before the Altar of Mithras. The Goths had seven deities: Sun, Moon, Tuisco, Woden, Thor, Friga, and Seatur or Saturn, from which we derive the names of the seven days of our week. In the Gothic mysteries the candidate met with seven obstructions. The ancient Jews swore by seven, because seven witnesses were used to confirm, and seven sacrifices offered to attest truth. The Sabbath is the seventh day; Noah had seven days' notice of the flood; God created the heaven and the earth in six days and rested on the seventh day; the walls of Jericho were encompassed seven times by seven priests bearing seven rams' horns; the Temple was seven years in building, and so on through a thousand references.

It is only necessary to refer to the seven necessary to open an Entered Apprentice's lodge, the seven original officers of a lodge (some now have nine or ten or even more) and the seven steps which complete the Winding Stairs to show that seven is an important number in the Fraternity.

THE SEVEN LIBERAL ARTS AND SCIENCES

In William Preston's day a liberal education was comprised in the study of grammar, rhetoric and logic, called the *trivium,* and arithmetic, geometry, music, and astronomy, called the *quadrivium.* Preston endeavored to compress into his Middle Chamber lecture enough of these to make at least an outline available to men who might otherwise know nothing of them.

In our day and times grammar and rhetoric are considered of importance, but in a secondary way; logic is more or less swallowed up as a study in the reasoning appropriate to any particular subject; arithmetic, of course, continues its primary importance; but from the standpoint of science, geometry and its offshoots are still the vital sciences of measurement. Music has fallen into the discard as part of a liberal education; it is now one of the arts, not the sciences, and astronomy is so interrelated with physics that it is hard to say where one leaves off and the other begins. As for electricity, chemistry, biology, civics, government, and the physical sciences, they were barely dreamed of in Preston's day.

So it is not actually but symbolically that we are to climb the seven steps. If the author may venture to quote himself:[1]

> William Preston, who put so practical an interpretation upon these steps, lived in an age when these did indeed represent all knowledge. But we must not refuse to grow because the ritual has not grown with modern discovery. When we rise by Grammar and Rhetoric, we must consider that they mean not only language, but all methods of communication. The step of Logic means a knowledge not only of a method of

[1] "*Foreign Countries,*" 1925.

reasoning, but of all reasoning which logicians have accomplished. When we ascend by Arithmetic and Geometry, we must visualize all science; since science is but measurement, in the true mathematical sense, it requires no great stretch of the imagination to read into these two steps all that science may teach. The step denominated Music means not only sweet and harmonious sounds, but all beauty—poetry, art, nature, loveliness of whatever kind. Not to be familiar with the beauty which nature provides is to be, by so much, less a man; to stunt, by so much, a starving soul. As for the seventh step of Astronomy, surely it means not only a study of the solar system and the stars as it did in William Preston's day, but also a study of all that is beyond the earth; of spirit and the world of spirit, of ethics, philosophy, the abstract—of Deity. Preston builded better than he knew; his seven steps are both logical in arrangement and suggestive in their order. The true Fellowcraft will see in them a guide to the making of a man rich in mind and spirit, by which riches only can true brotherhood be practiced.

THE STAIRS WIND

Finally consider the implications of the *winding* stairs, as opposed to those which are straight.

The one virtue which most distinguishes man is courage. It requires more courage to face the unknown than the known. A straight stair, a ladder, hides neither secret nor mystery at its top. But the stairs which wind hide each step from the climber; what is just around the corner is unknown. The winding stairs of life lead us to we know not what; for some of us a Middle Chamber of fame and fortune; for others, one of pain and frustration. The Angel of Death may stand with drawn sword on the very next step for any of us.

Yet man climbs.

Man has always climbed; he climbed from a cave man savagery to the dawn of civilization; Lowell's

. . . brute despair of trampled centuries,
Leapt up with one hoarse yell and snapped its bands;
Groped for its right with horny, callous hands
And stared around for God with bloodshot eyes,

was a climbing from slavery to independence, from the brutish to the spiritual. Through ignorance, darkness, misery, cruelty, wrong, oppression, danger, and despair, man has climbed to enlightenment. Each individual man must climb his little winding stairs through much the same experience as that of the race.

Aye, man climbs because he has courage; because he has faith; because he is a *man.* So must the Freemason climb. The winding stairs *do* lead somewhere. There *is* a Middle Chamber. There *are* wages of the Fellowcraft to be earned.

So believing, so, unafraid, climbing, the Fellowcraft may hope at the top of his winding stairs to reach a Middle Chamber, and see a new sign in the East . . .

LETTER "G"

Its first reference is to the first and noblest of the sciences, geometry. Geometry, the fifth of the

Seven Liberal Arts and Sciences, and astronomy, the seventh science, are so much a part of each other that it is difficult to consider them separately; indeed, the ritual of the letter "G" is as much concerned with the study of the heavens as of the science of measurement alone. We hear:

> By it we discover the power, the wisdom, and the goodness of the Grand Artificer of the Universe and view with delight the wonderful proportions of this vast machine. By it we discover how the planets move in their respective orbits and demonstrate their various revolutions. . . . Numberless worlds are around us, all framed by the same Divine Artist, which roll through the vast expanse, controlled by the same unerring law.

It is difficult to visualize the vital importance of the heavens to early men. We can hardly conceive of their terror of the eclipse and the comet or sense their veneration for the Sun and his bride, the Moon. We are too well educated. We know too much about "the proportions which connect this vast machine." The astronomer has pushed back the frontiers of his science beyond the comprehension of most of us; the questions which occur as a result of unaided visual observations have all been answered. We have substituted facts for fancies regarding the sun, the moon, the solar system, the comet, and the eclipse.

Pike[1] says:

[1] Albert Pike: born 1809, died 1891. One of the greatest geniuses Freemasonry has ever known. It is said of him that "he found Scottish Rite Masonry in a hovel and left it in a palace." He was a mystic, a symbolist, a teacher

FELLOWCRAFT

We cannot, even in the remotest degree, feel, though we may partially and imperfectly imagine, how those great, primitive, simple-hearted children of Nature felt in regard to the Starry Hosts, there upon the slopes of the Himalayas, on the Chaldean plains, in the Persian and Median deserts, and upon the banks of the great, strange river, the Nile. To them the Universe was alive—instinct with forces and powers, mysterious and beyond their comprehension. To them it was no machine, no great system of clockwork; but a great live creature, in sympathy with or inimical to man. To them, all was mystery and a miracle, and the stars flashing overhead spoke to their hearts almost in an audible language. Jupiter, with its kingly splendors, was the emperor of the starry legions. Venus looked lovingly on the earth and blessed it; Mars with his crimson fires threatened war and misfortune; and Saturn, cold and grave, chilled and repelled them. The ever-changing Moon, faithful companion of the Sun, was a constant miracle and wonder; the Sun himself the visible emblem of the creative and generative power. To them the earth was a great plain, over which the sun, the moon and the planets revolved, its servants, framed to give it light. Of the stars, some were beneficent existences that brought with them springtime and fruits and flowers—some, faithful sentinels, advising them of coming inundation, of the season of storm and of deadly winds;

of the hidden truths of Freemasonry. To him the world of Freemasonry owes a debt of incalculable size. Poet, Freemason, philosopher, his genius had a profound effect upon the Craft in general, and the Ancient Accepted Scottish Rite of Freemasonry in particular.

> some heralds of evil, which, steadily foretelling, they seemed to cause. To them the eclipses were portents of evil, and their causes hidden in mystery, and supernatural. The regular returns of the stars, the comings of Arcturus, Orion, Sirius, the Pleiades, and Aldebaran, and the journeyings of the Sun, were voluntary and not mechanical to them. What wonder that astronomy became to them the most important of sciences; that those who learned it became rulers; and that vast edifices, the Pyramids, the tower or temple of Bel, and other like erections elsewhere in the East, were builded for astronomical purposes?—and what wonder that, in their great childlike simplicity, they worshiped Light, the Sun. the Planets, and the Stars, and personified them, and eagerly believed in the histories invented for them; in that age when the capacity for belief was infinite; as indeed, if we but reflect, it still is and ever will be?

Anglo-Saxons usually consider history as their history; science as their science; religion as their religion. This somewhat naïve viewpoint is hardly substantiated by a less egoistic survey of knowledge. Columbus' sailors believed they would fall off the edge of a flat world, yet Pythagoras knew the earth to be a ball. The ecliptic was known before Solomon's Temple was built; the Chinese predicted eclipses long, long before the Europeans of the Middle Ages regarded them as portents of doom!

Astronomical lore in Freemasonry is very old. The foundations of our degrees are far more ancient than we can prove by documentary evidence. It is surely not stretching credulity to believe that the study which antedates geometry must have been impressed on our Order, its ceremonies and its symbols, long before Preston and Webb worked their ingenious revolutions in our rituals and gave us the system of degrees we use to-day in one form or another.

The astronomical references in our degrees begin with the points of the compass; East, West, and South, and the place of darkness, the North. We are taught why the North is a place of darkness by the position of Solomon's Temple with reference to the ecliptic, a most important astronomical conception. The sun is the Past Master's own symbol; our Masters rule their lodges—or are supposed to! —with the same regularity with which the sun rules the day and the moon governs the night. Our explanation of our Lesser Lights is obviously an adaptation of a concept which dates back to the earliest of religions; specifically to the Egyptian Isis, Osiris, and Horus, represented by the sun, moon, and Mercury.

In circumambulation about the altar we traverse our lodges from East to West by way of the South as did the sun worshipers who thus imitated the daily passage of their deity through the heavens.

Measures of time are astronomical. Days and nights were before man and consequently before astronomy but hours and minutes are inventions of the mind, depending upon the astronomical observation of the sun at meridian to determine noon and consequently all other periods of time. The Middle Chamber work gives to geometry the premier place as a means by which the astronomer may fix the duration of time and seasons, years and cycles.

Observing that the sun rose and set our ancient brethren easily determined East and West, although as the sun rises and sets through a variation of 47 degrees north and south during a six months' period the determination was not exact.

The earliest Chaldean star gazers, progenitors of the astronomers of later ages, saw that the apparently revolving heavens pivoted on a point nearly coincident with a certain star. We know that the true north diverges from the North Star one and a half degrees, but their observations were sufficiently accurate to determine a North—and consequently East, West, and South.

A curious derivation of a Masonic symbol from the heavens is that universally associated with the Stewards, the cornucopia.

According to the mythology of the Greeks which goes back to the very dawn of civilization, the god Zeus was nourished in infancy from the milk of the goat, Amalthea. In gratitude the god placed Amalthea forever in the heavens as a constellation, but first he gave one of Amalthea's horns to his nurses with the assurance that it would forever pour for them whatever they desired.

The horn of plenty, or the cornucopia, is thus a symbol of abundance. The goat from which it came may be found by the curious among the constellations under the name of Capricorn. The Tropic of Capricorn of our school days is the southern limit of the swing of the sun on the path which marks the ecliptic, on which the earth dips first its north, then its south pole toward our luminary. Hence there is a connection, not the less direct for being tenuous, between our Stewards, their symbol, the lights in the lodge, the place of darkness, and Solomon's Temple.

Of such curious links and interesting bypaths is the connection of astronomy with geometry and the letter "G," the more beautiful when we see eye to eye with the Psalmist: "The heavens declare the glory of God and the firmament sheweth his handiwork."

"GOD IS ALWAYS GEOMETRIZING"

So said Plato twenty-three centuries ago. It is merely an accident of the English language that geometry and God begin with the same letter; no matter what the language or the ritual, the initial of the Ineffable Name and that of the first and noblest of sciences are Masonically the same.

"But that is secret!" cries some newly-initiated brother who has examined his printed monitor and finds that the ritual concerning the further significance of the letter "G" is represented only by stars. Aye, the *ritual* is secret, but the *fact* is the most gloriously public that Freemasonry may herald to the world. One can no more keep secret the idea that God is the very warp and woof of Freemasonry than that He is the essence of all life. Take God out of Freemasonry and there is, literally, nothing left; it is a pricked balloon, an empty vessel, a bubble which has burst.

The petitioner knows it before he signs his application. He must answer "Do you believe in God?" before his petition can be accepted. He must declare his faith in a Supreme Being before he may be initiated. But note that he is not required to say, then or ever, *what* God. He may name Him as he will, think of Him as he pleases; make Him impersonal law or personal and anthropomorphic; Freemasonry cares not.

Freemasonry's own especial name for Deity is Great Architect of the Universe. She speaks of God rarely as if she felt the sacredness of the simple Jewish symbol—the Yod—which stood for JHVH, that unpronouncable name we think may have been Jehovah. But God, Great Architect of the Universe, Grand Artificer, Grand Master of the Grand Lodge Above, Jehovah, Allah, Buddha, Brahma, Vishnu, Shiva, or Great Geometer, a symbol of the conception shines in the East of every American Masonic lodge, as in the center of the canopy of every English lodge.

Secret? Aye, secret as those matters of the heart which may not be told are secret. Let him who loves his wife or his child more than he loves aught else upon the earth try to explain in words just how he loves, and he will understand just what sort of a secret this is. All the world may know *that* he loves; *how* he loves, how *much* he loves, there are no words to tell.

All the world may know that the symbol of Deity shines in the East of a Masonic lodge; only the true Freemason, who is actually a Mason in his heart, as well as in his mind, may know just how and in what way the Great Architect is the very essence and substance of the Ancient Craft.

The symbol of Deity has always been a part of all houses of initiation. In the Egyptian mysteries it was the Sun God's symbol, *Ra*. The Greeks considered the number five to be the symbol of man's dependence upon the Unseen; from five also came the Pentalpha or five-pointed star. The imaginative will easily see here a connection with the Fellowcraft's Degree in which five is especially the symbolic number. Plutarch tells us that in the Greek mysteries the symbol of God was made of wood in the first, of bronze in the second, and of gold in the third degree, or step, to symbolize the refinement of man's conception of Deity as he progressed from the darkness of ignorance to the light of faith in some one of many forms of belief in God.

Freemasonry uses a much more tender and beautiful symbolism. In modern and costly temples the letter "G" may be of crystal, lighted behind with electric light. In some country lodge it may be cut from cardboard and painted blue, illuminated if at all with a tallow dip. A Western lodge meets yearly on the top of a hill in a forest, and nails to a tree cut branches in the form of a rough letter "G." Freemasonry's symbolism is not of the material substance of the letter, but its connection with geometry, the science by which the universe exists and moves and by which the proportions which connect this vast machine are measured.

Aye, God is always geometrizing. Geometry is particularly His science. Freemasonry makes it especially the science of the Fellowcraft's Degree and couples it with the symbol of the Great Architect of the Universe. No teaching of Freemasonry is greater; none is simpler than this. The Fellowcraft who sees it as the very crux and climax of the degree, the reality behind the form, has learned as no words may teach him for what he climbed the Winding Stairs, and the true wages of a Fellowcraft which he found within the Middle Chamber.

HISTORY—THE GRAND LODGE PERIOD

The formation of the Mother Grand Lodge in London, in 1717, which profoundly affected Freemasonry, is shrouded in mystery, clouded in the mists of time, and as extraordinary as it was important.

The Freemasons of those far-off days could have had no idea of the tremendous issues which hung upon their actions nor dreamed of the effect of their union. Had they even imagined it, doubtless they would have left us more records, and we would not now have to speculate on matters of history the very causes of which are—in all probability—never fully to be known to us.

One of the causes which led to the sudden coming to life of the old and diminishing Fraternity was the Reformation. During its operative period Freemasonry had been if not a child of the Church at least its servant, working hand in hand with it. Our oldest document—the Halliwell Manuscript or Regius Poem, dated 1390—invokes the Virgin Mary, speaks of the Trinity and gives instructions for observing Mass! But the same influences which produced the Reformation worked in Freemasonry and by 1600, according to the Harleian Manuscript,[1] the Order had

[1] Harleian Manuscript: dated about the middle of the Seventeenth Century and originally the property of Robert Harley, Earl of Oxford.

largely severed its dependence upon the Church and become a refuge for those who wished to be free in thought as well as for Freemasons. It was still Christian—almost aggressively Christian—in its teachings. Not for another hundred years or more and then only partially did it rid itself of any sectarian character whatever and become what it is to-day, a meeting ground for "men of every country, sect and opinion," united in a common belief in the Fatherhood of God, the brotherhood of man, and the hope of immortality.

Seventeen hundred and seventeen is the dividing line between before and after; between the old Freemasonry and the new; between a Craft which was slowly expiring and one which began to grow with a new vitality; between the last lingering remains of operative Masonry and a Craft wholly Speculative.

Just what were the causes of the events which led up to the formation of the first Grand Lodge we do not know. We can only guess. No minutes of the Mother Grand Lodge were kept during its first six years. The Constitutions and Old Charges, first published in 1723, were republished fifteen years after. In this second edition of 1738 is a meager record of the first meetings of the Grand Lodge, so brief and so skeletonized that there is space for it in such a little book as this. In the yellowed pages of this old and precious book of which a few copies still remain we read (letters modernized):

> King George I entered London most magnificently on 20 Sept., 1714, and after the Rebellion was over 1716 A.D., the few Lodges at

London finding themselves neglected by Sir Christopher Wren, thought fit to cement under a Grand Master as the Center of Union and Harmony, viz., the Lodges that met,

1. At the Goose and Gridiron Alehouse at St. Pauls Church-yard.
2. At the Crown Alehouse in Parker's-Lane, near Drury-Lane.
3. At the Apple-Tree Tavern in Charles-street, Covent Garden.
4. At the Rummer and Grapes Tavern in Channel-Row, Westminster.

They and some old Brothers met at the said Apple-Tree, and having put in the chair the oldest Master Mason (now the Master of a Lodge) they constituted themselves a Grand Lodge *pro Tempore* in due form, and forthwith revived the Quarterly Communication of the Officers of Lodges (called the Grand Lodge) resolved to hold the Annual Assembly and Feast and then to chuse a Grand Master from among themselves, till they should have the Honor of a Noble Brother at their Head.

Accordingly on St. John Baptist's Day, in the 3d year of King George I. A.D. 1717 the Assembly and Feast of the Free and accepted Masons was held at the foresaid Goose and Gridiron Ale-house.

Before Dinner, the oldest Master Mason (now the Master of a Lodge) in the Chair, proposed a List of proper Candidates; and the Brethren by a Majority of Hands elected Mr. Anthony Sayer Gentleman, Grand Master of Masons—Capt. Joseph Elliot, Mr. Jacob Lamball, Carpenter, Grand Wardens—who being forthwith invested with the Badges of Office and power by the said oldest Master, and installed, was duly congratulated by the Assembly who paid him the Homage.

Sayer Grand Master commanded the Masters and Wardens of Lodges to meet the Grand Officers every Quarter in Communication at the place he should appoint in his Summons sent by the Tyler.

N. B. It is called the Quarterly Communication, because it should meet Quarterly according to ancient Usage. And when the Grand Master is present it is a Lodge in Ample Form; otherwise, only in Due Form, yet having the same authority with Ample Form.

Probably other lodges existed in London at the time; whether they refused to join the historic four or were not invited we do not know. We know little about these original four lodges. The Engraved List of Lodges was published in 1729 in which the Goose and Gridiron Number 1 (afterwards the Lodge of Antiquity) is said to have dated from 1691. When William Preston became its Master the lodge was involved in a controversy with the Grand Lodge—but that is too special an event to consider in so broad a sketch as this.

Lodge number two of the original four lodges, which met at the Crown, Parker's-Lane, was struck from the roll in 1740. The first Grand Master of this Mother Grand Lodge, Anthony Sayer, Gentleman, came from lodge number three—the Apple-Tree Tavern Lodge; we know little more of it. These three lodges were small, and at least as much operative as Speculative. But the fourth lodge, which met at the Rummer and Grapes Tavern in Channel Row, Westminster, was not only the largest (seventy members) but the most Speculative and with the highest type of membership. It mothered not only men of high social rank, lords, counts and knights, but also Dr. Desaguliers[1] and James Anderson,[2] two brethren who had a great deal to do with the revival, especially Anderson, to whom we are indebted for much.

In our perspective a Grand Lodge is as much a necessary part of the existing order of things as a State or Federal Government. In 1717 it was a new idea, accompanied by many other new ideas. Some brother or brethren saw that if the ancient Order were not to die, it must be given new life through a new organization. Doubtless they were influenced by Mother Kilwinning Lodge[3] of Scotland which had

[1] John Theophilus Desaguliers, LL.D. F.R.S., born 1683, died 1744, sometimes called the Father of Modern Speculative Masonry. He was the third Grand Master of the first Grand Lodge and thrice afterwards Deputy Grand Master. He is credited with having been the inspiration of Anderson, and to have supplied much of the material from which Anderson wrote his "Constitutions."

[2] James Anderson, Father of the first printed Constitutions, 1723, which contains the Old Charges, the General Regulations, and a fanciful, fascinating, but wholly erroneous history of Freemasonry.

[3] Kilwinning: a small town in Scotland which tradition states is the birthplace of Freemasonry in the land of heather, as is York the seat of the first General Assembly of Freemasons in England. Kilwinning Lodge—Mother Kilwinning by affection and common consent—at one time seceded from the Mother Grand Lodge, during which period she chartered various lodges as of "inherent right," including one in Virginia in 1785.

assumed and exercised certain motherly functions in regard to her daughter lodges, all of which had Kilwinning as a part of their name and, apparently, of their obedience.

The newly formed Grand Lodge went the whole way. It proposed to, and did, take command of its lodges. It branched out beyond the jurisdiction originally proposed "within ten miles of London" and invaded the provinces. It gave enormous powers to the Grand Master. It prohibited the working of the "Master's Part" in private lodges, thus throwing back to the ancient annual assemblies.[1] It divided the Craft into Entered Apprentices and Fellowcrafts. It resolved "against all politics as what never yet conduced to the welfare of the lodge nor ever will." This was a highly important declaration at a time when every organization in England was taking part in politics, especially in the Jacobite struggle against the House of Hanover. Indeed, a Grand Master, the Duke of Wharton (1722) turned against the Grand Lodge and the Fraternity when it refused to lend itself to his political aspirations and sponsored the Gormogons, a caricature organization which tried to destroy Freemasonry by

[1] Assembly: sometimes called General Assembly, or Yearly Assembly. The word seems to denote a meeting of Masons in the ancient operative days equivalent to a modern lodge. The York Manuscript No. 1, dated approximately 1600, says: "Edwin procured of ye King his father a charter and commission to holde every yeare an assembly wheresoever they would within ye realm of England." In the Harleian Manuscript, 1660, it is set forth that: ". . . every Master and Fellow come to the Assembly, if it be within five miles about him, if he have any warning."

ridicule. Luckily for us all, ridicule, powerful weapon though it is, never in the long run prevails against reality. The Gormogons, like other and later organizations, such as the Scald Miserable Masons,[1] had its brief day and died—and Freemasonry throve and grew.

Finally the Grand Lodge erased the ancient Charge "to be true to God and Holy Church" and substituted the Charge already quoted (*see* page 39).

This was of unparalleled importance; it was one of the factors which led to the formation of other Grand Lodges and dissension in Freemasonry, but as it was distinctly *right* and founded modern speculative Freemasonry on the rock of non-sectarianism and the brotherhood of all men who believe in a common Father regardless of His name, His church, or the way in which He is worshiped, it won out in the end and became what it is to-day, a fundamental of the Craft.

Between 1717 and 1751 the Craft spread rapidly, not only in England, but on the Continent, and in the Colonies, especially Colonial America, where time and people, conditions and social life provided fallow ground for the seeds of Freemasonry. But in spite of a new life, and wise counsels of brethren

[1] Scald Miserables: mock Masons who paraded in London in 1741. Many such mock Masonic processions were formed by enemies of the Order—often men who had been denied acceptance. Of little importance then, and none now, except that the Masonic disinclination to take part in public processions—dedications, cornerstone layings and funerals excepted—comes from the mock Masonic processions which imitated the ancient "March of Procession" of Masons in London in the early years of the Grand Lodge.

who restricted the acts if not the power of the new Grand Lodge, all was not plain sailing. Dissensions appeared. Causes of friction, if not numerous, were important and went deep. The religious issue was vital; doubtless it seemed to the older Masons then as radical a step as it seemed to us when the Grand Orient of France[1] took the V. S. L. from the altar. In the 1738 edition of the Constitutions we find the article "Concerning God and religion" altered to read, "In ancient times the *Christian* Masons were charged to comply with the *Christian* usages of each country where they traveled and worked."

Another cause for dissension was the Grand Lodge's strong hand regarding the making of Masons. Too many lodges were careless; too many private groups of Masons assumed the right to assemble as a lodge and make Masons of their friends; too much laxity existed as to fees and dues and the payment of charity to the Grand Lodge. To check these practices the Grand Lodge changed some words in the degrees—doubtless our "spurious Mason" clauses come from this—and this caused the same reaction then as an attempt by modern brethren to change or rearrange our present ritual would produce.

Probably the religious issue did not cause a major

[1] Grand Orient of France: a body once Masonic which is without recognition by the Grand Lodges of England, the United States, and most of the other nations. It removed from its Constitutions a paragraph affirming the existence of the Great Architect of the Universe. Withdrawal of recognition by the United Grand Lodge of England followed immediately (1878) and ever since the Grand Orient has been clandestine to practically all the Masonic world.

part of the trouble, but it provided a constant source of irritation. Then as now many clergymen were Speculative Masons. To-day enlightened clergymen do not see in the absence of mention of the Carpenter of Nazareth in a lodge any denial of Him, any more than a Jewish Rabbi sees in the absence of mention of Jehovah, or a Buddhist sees in the absence of mention of Buddha, a denial of those deities. Then, however, many clergymen insisted upon a Christian tinge to the Masonic ceremonies, and while the quarrel would hardly have come from this alone, it was a contributing cause.

In 1738 the Grand Lodge *sanctioned* the making of the "Master's Part" into what we know as the Third Degree. This had been going on for years —no one knows how many—but not by permission of Grand Lodge. Sanctioning it was to many brethren an "alteration of established usage" and the customs of "time immemorial." It proved another blow struck at unity.

All these and other matters fomented dissension which came to a head in 1751 when a rival Grand Lodge was formed. It came into being with a brilliant stroke, for it chose the name "The Most Antient and Honorable Fraternity of Free and Accepted Masons."

Calling itself "Antient" and the older body "Modern" at once enlisted the support of hundreds of brethren who did not look beneath the surface to learn which was really which. So we have this peculiar and confusing terminology; the original, the older, the more ancient Grand Lodge was called the "Modern" Grand Lodge, and the newer and rebellious body was called "Antient."[1]

The curious story of the rise of this Antient Grand Lodge should be read by every Freemason, for it has had a tremendous effect upon the Craft. We can afford to be charitable to those who believed they were engaged in a revolution, not a rebellion. This country was born out of what we call the Revolution, which to the Royalists of 1776 was the Rebellion.

The Antients were extremely fortunate in having one Laurence Dermott secede from the Moderns with them. Dermott was a fighting Irishman, a brother heart and soul in the Fraternity, and if some of his actions seem a little questionable to us, he has to his credit the success of the movement. In 1771 when the Duke of Atholl became Grand Master the Antients had almost two hundred lodges on the roll.

Dermott kept the religious issue alive; by implication he made the Moderns seem anti-religious. He

[1] United States Grand Lodges style themselves under several different abbreviations: F. and A. M.; A. F. and A. M., and variations using the Ampersand (&) in place of the word "and." The District of Columbia still uses F. A. A. M., meaning Free and Accepted Masons, in spite of the possible confusion as to whether the first A stands for "and" or "ancient." The variations are accounted for by differences in origins, some Grand Lodges coming into being with lodges which held under the "Ancients," and some from the "Moderns," and by variations due to the errors which are seemingly ineradicable in "mouth-to-ear" instruction. Whether Ancient Free and Accepted Masons; Free, Ancient and Accepted Masons; Ancient Free Masons, or any other combination of the words, all United States Grand Lodges are "regular," tracing descent either mediately or immediately to the United Grand Lodge of England and recognized by her.

kept the Antients a Christian body and wrote distinctively Christian sentiments and references into its Constitutions and its documents whenever he could get them adopted.

Meanwhile other Grand Lodges arose; they were not very important and never grew very large, but they belong in the story of Freemasonry; the "Grand Lodge of All England," "The Grand Lodge of England South of the River Trent," "The Supreme Grand Lodge" all made their bids for recognition, lived their little day and passed on, each leaving its trace, its influence, but unable to contend against the Antients and the Moderns.

The benefits which came from the clash seem to-day to be greater than the evils. Then Freemasons saw only harm in the rivalry which split the Fraternity. Now we can see that where one Grand Lodge established lodges on war-ships, the other retaliated with Army lodges which carried Freemasonry to far places; where one body started a school for girls, the other retorted with a school for boys—both still in existence, by the way—where one Grand Lodge reached out to the provinces, the other cultivated Scotland and Ireland. Both worked indefatigably in the American Colonies.

The heart burnings, the jealousies, the sorrows and the contests between Antients and Moderns, if they exhibited less of brotherly love than the Fraternity taught, were actually spurs to action. Without some such urge Freemasonry could hardly have spread so fast or so far. As the United States became a much stronger and more closely welded union after the cleavage of 1861–65, so Freemasonry was to unite at last in a far greater, stronger and more harmonious body when the two rival Grand Lodges came together, composed their differences, forgot their rivalries, and clasped hands across the altar of the United Grand Lodge.

The reconciliation is as astonishing and mysterious as the discord. We can see that the death of Dermott, who was gathered to his fathers in 1791, fighting for the Antients to the last, removed one cause of difference between the two Grand Lodges; we can understand that as the Antients had grown in power and prestige not only in England but in the Colonies until they outnumbered the Moderns in both lodges and brethren, the Moderns might well have thought that union would be a life saver; we can comprehend that time heals all differences and that what had seemed important in 1751 in fifty years had dwindled in vitality.

But what is amazing to this day is that after the difficult period, when overtures were made, refusals recorded, committees appointed and differences finally composed, the Antient Grand Lodge, in accepting the idea of reconciliation, *receded from almost all the positions for which it had fought so long!* It was as if the spirit of combat, so alien to the gentle genius of Freemasonry, had worn itself out and brethren became as eager to forgive and forget and compromise as they had previously been strong to resist and to struggle.

Whatever the spirit which caused it, the final reconciliation took place in Freemasons' Hall in London, on St. John's Day, December 27, 1813. The two Grand Lodges filed together into the Hall; the

Articles of Union were read; the Duke of Kent retired as Grand Master in favor of the Duke of Sussex, who was elected Grand Master of the United Grand Lodge.

Two matters must be stressed: the second of the Articles of Union reads: "It is declared and pronounced that pure ancient Masonry consists of three degrees and no more; viz., those of the Entered Apprentice, the Fellowcraft and the Master Mason (including the Supreme Order of the Holy Royal Arch)."

In 1815 a new Book of Constitutions proclaimed to all the world forever the non-sectarian character of Freemasonry in this Charge concerning God and religion:

"Let a man's religion or mode of worship be what it may, he is not excluded from the Order, provided he believes in the glorious Architect of heaven and earth, and practice the sacred duties of morality."

Newton says of this:

> Surely that is broad enough, high enough; and we ought to join with it the famous proclamation issued by the Grand Master, the Duke of Sussex, from Kensington Palace, in 1842, declaring that Masonry is not identified with any one religion to the exclusion of others, and men in India who were otherwise eligible and could make a sincere profession of faith in one living God, be they Hindus or Mohammedans, might petition for membership in the Craft. Such in our own day is the spirit and practice of Masonic universality, and from that position, we may be very sure, the Craft will never recede.

Printed in Great
Britain
by Amazon

32102642R00040